Eden Glen

The Last Unicorn

I0571169

Author: Bruce Nadeau

Illustrator: Bruce Nadeau

Publisher: Jeffrey McGraw

Presented by:
Nadeau Press,BNJM

Find Nadeau Press on
Facebook and Twitter

The Worlds of Nadeau Press:

Babru the Pirate:

    The Silver Pipe Adventure

    Search for the Orange Obelisk

    The Wedding Day Tale

    The Riddle of the Sphinx

Eden Glen Chronicles:

    The Last Unicorn

    The Great Sea Dragon

The Calabash Kids Adventures:

    The Dragon's Claw

    The Time Machine

Acknowledgements

This book is dedicated to my little horse fairy Zayana, and her train building gnome brother Simon! Thank you for reminding me everyday...MAGIC IS REAL!

Thank you to Nadine, "my dearest", for allowing me to let my imagination run away...

And finally to Robin. A finer grammar troll there has never been. Yes, I am aware commas were invented for a reason!

Nadeau Press
BNJM

Copyright © 2015 BNJM
ISBN-13: 978-0692600450

ISBN-10: 0692600450

1

There is a land that every child has seen, but that none have ever visited. It is a land that is found between the spot where imagination ends, and dreams begin. A land that is home to all manner of beings that children know in their hearts are real, and adults are sure never existed. A place where all four seasons occur at the same time and life thrives above the ground and below the sea. A land of beauty, wonder, and perhaps most important of all, a land of MAGIC!

This is the fantastical world of Eden Glen. A beautiful valley located between a range of un-climbable mountains, and an un-crossable lake. It lies behind an impenetrable forest, and above an un-passable snow line. It is a home to a world of friendship and wonder. Eden Glen is home to dragons, gnomes, elves, trolls, mermaids, animals of any imagining, and fairies.

Life in Eden Glen is actually quite like the lives that you and I live every day. Creatures of all kinds get up every morning and begin their days. Fairies head off to their jobs caring for all manner of animals that call Eden Glen their home. Gnomes go into their gardens to tend every type of plant that you can imagine. Elves patrol the forest pruning dead tree branches, harvesting syrup, and picking the occasional pine cone. Trolls keep maintenance of roads and bridges. And mermaids and mermen do all of the same things, only under the sea.

And, of course, the children of all type

play together, and head off to learn their lessons together too. There was a time however, when this was not the case. Not so long ago a fairy born to parents that were squirrel fairies had no choice but to care for squirrels. A broccoli gnome's son could grow only broccoli, even if he did prefer spinach. But that all changed when Jeremiah Terrificus Shodbottom became an advisor to the Council of Elders. Jeremiah Terrificus, known simply as JT to his friends, is perhaps the most famous and influential gnome the world has ever known.

As much as JT loved life in Eden Glen, he was curious about life beyond its borders. So as a young gnome, JT left the Glen to explore the human world. What he discovered was beyond anything he could have thought possible. Being careful to stay hidden, he marveled at the world in which these creatures lived. They traveled in horseless coaches that moved faster than he could see. He saw great birds that carried humans in their bellies, and flew without flapping their wings. And they lived in great buildings that at night were lit by candles with no flame.

JT did his best to stay out of sight, but one night in London, he had a great impact on a young artist who lived there. Usually traveling at night, JT had selected a quiet garden in a quiet neighborhood to sleep away the day. When he awoke however, he realized just how rundown the garden had become, and following his natural instincts, he began to prune and care for a neglected hydrangea bush. What JT did not know though, was that his efforts did not go unnoticed. He was so intent on his work, he never noticed the fluttering curtains in the second story bedroom window of the small flat. A young man, an artist who lost his inspiration, sat watching in wonder night after night as JT turned the overrun patch of weeds into a beautifully flowered and fountained display.

When JT strode confidently out of his hiding spot for his final night of pruning and planting, he was quite shocked to find the artist sitting next to the fountain with tears in his eyes. As JT began to flee, the young man pled with him to stop.

"Oh please, mysterious creature. Whoever or whatever you are, don't run away. I'm so very sad and the only joy I have found, no matter how fleeting, has been in watching your artistry." He wiped his eyes, choked back a sob, and then continued. "I'm supposed to

4

be an artist, but I have no great ideas. No inspirations. The only time that I have been happy has been in watching you take this overgrown patch of weeds, and make them into a place of peace and beauty. And now you are done and are leaving. And I will never see you again!"

The young man's head fell forward onto his arms and he sobbed. As he cried JT walked quietly to the shed in the garden that he used as a studio, swept off weeks of cobwebs that had gathered from lack of use, and went inside. He emerged moments later pulling a small wagon with a block of modeling clay atop it. JT stopped in front of the young man, and without saying a word (to this day no one is really sure if humans can understand gnomes speak) put his hands on his knee and smiled into his wet tear streaked face. He pointed to the clay, stepped back, put one hand on his hip, and pointed his other at the plant. He then stood there perfectly still.

The man just looked at him for a moment, and then understood what was expected. He plunged his hands into the clay, and began to squeeze and shape. He worked until his hands cramped and his shoulders ached, and then worked even more. When the sun began to rise, he looked down at a perfect representation of the small gnome made of grey modeling clay. He lay down his head with the intention of just resting his eyes for a few moments, and fell into a deep and happy sleep. As he slept JT patted his head, and then left the garden.

Having decided it was time for him to return to Eden Glen, JT chose to visit that garden one last time before he left. When he arrived he found that the statue of him was painted in the same color clothing that he had worn on that night, including the pointy red cap that he had on his head. The statue had been placed under that hydrangea he first started working with, and he could not help but to feel proud of the rich colorful blossoms that now adorned the shrub. Next to the statue was a note written to him. JT could not read the words (English being as foreign to him as gnomes speak would be to the artist) but he knew a thank you when he saw it.

As he left the garden for the final time, he walked up the avenue and noticed similar statues, in different colored clothes, in no less than five gardens. The artist had found his inspiration, and JT became the most famous gnome that has ever lived. Any time you see a garden gnome statue near your home, what you are actually looking at is a statue of Mr. Jeremiah Terrificus Shodbottom!

During his time in the outside world, JT learned a very important lesson as well. He noticed that humans, especially children, didn't keep entirely to their own kind. He noted that children did not care that other children did not look like them; they were still children and therefore, fun to play with. Boys and girls, dark skin and light skin, tall and short, thin or heavy, did not matter.

And they didn't all do what their parents did either. They attended classes together, and learned things that their parents did not know, and they were all happy. He also appreciated that the children's educators helped them to learn things that made them happy. When he finally returned to Eden Glen, the first thing he did was bring this information to the Council of Elders.

Moved by JT's words and his stories about the world of humans, the Council of Elders decided to open the Eden Glen School for Different Knowledge. The EGSDK as it was known, encouraged learning in all children that called Eden Glen home. If a student wished, he or she could learn new skills no matter what the profession of their parents.

That is how JT became Professor Shodbottom, Headmaster and Dean of the EGSDK, and he truly loved his job. As the oldest son of a potato gnome, becoming a teacher meant that he was the first member of Eden Glen Society to choose his own career. That he could now help others do the same thing thrilled him. Nothing made him happier than teaching, and he felt no greater joy than seeing his students learn.

2

Eliza Thistlewhite fluttered her small fairy wings as fast as she could, trying her best to keep up with the huge steps that her professor took. The Thistlewhites were a family of bunny fairies, but Eliza knew in her heart that she was meant for much, much more. That was why she found herself flitting through the Great

Guardian Forest on this cold drizzly morning, following behind a huge muscular ogre.

Seven students had begun the Dragon Studies program but Eliza, now in her third semester at the Eden Glen School for Different Knowledge, was the only student that remained in the class. Professor Slackjaw the Ogre, perhaps the greatest dragon wrangler the world has ever known, was the Dean of the Dragon Studies Department, as well as the Professor for Advanced Dragonry 101.

"Miss Thistlewhite," said the deep gravelly voice of Slackjaw. "Did you study your lessons last night?"

"Of course, Professor," replied the tiny fairy. "I read chapters seven through nine in the *Caring for Dragons* text, as well as the first three chapters of *Staring at the Beast*. Unless I'm mistaken Professor, you are the author of that book."

"Mm-hmm," said the ogre nodding his head.

Eliza thought back to her first day of class. It seemed so very long ago, and like it just happened at the same time. She arrived wearing her usual clothing, rhododendron petals woven together with rabbit fur. She felt very much out of place, and learned that style of outfit just would not work. She quickly made friends with a young troll named Aloysius who was in his second semester of clothing manufacturing. He made her a new outfit, not of flower petals like most fairies would wear, but of sturdy cottons and wools. They were much more fitting for the tough challenges of dragon wrangling.

Now she wore a gray wool hooded jacket with special vents sewn into the back to accommodate her wings. She wore a pair of blue denim pants with black leather knee high boots. Eliza bore a closer resemblance to the ogre that she traveled with, except for her size, than to other fairies. That didn't bother her however. She knew who she was and was very happy with it.

"Professor?" Eliza asked. "Your text said that handling a dragon was all in the look, but I'm not sure that I understand. Is it a stare? A glare?"

"No, Ms. Thistlewhite," said Slackjaw. He continued on never looking back, keeping the same brisk pace, his hands joined behind his back. At first glance ogres seem slow and clumsy, almost too big to be able to move.

Their deep graveled voices give them the impression of dimwittedness, and the heavy brows over deep set eyes are very misleading. Slackjaw the Ogre was muscular and very fast. He was one of the smartest teachers at the school, and only spoke slowly and quietly to keep from scaring his students.

"Eliza," he finally said while turning around and bending over. Eliza, fluttering with her head down, nearly collided with his huge nose. She slowly backed up and looked at his smile full of uneven teeth. "The look is not about how you fix your eyes, but the will that is conveyed by those eyes. The look is not about staring at, but staring into. The look immediately tells a dragon all that it needs to know."

"What it needs to know, sir?"

"Exactly. The look tells the dragon whether it should respect you...," Slackjaw stood straight and continued to follow the path through the forest and with a chuckle added, "... or eat you."

Eliza gulped to herself, and then fluttered quickly to catch up. While her reading and studying led to excellent grades in the classroom, today was going to be her first day working with a real dragon. She knew that it

would be a juvenile dragon, no older than she was in dragon years. Even though it would be much smaller than a full grown mature dragon, it would still seem gigantic as compared to the tiny fairy.

Eliza continued along, lost in her own thoughts. Her heart raced as she thought about the living animal she was about to face. As they wound up the path, she began to hear low growls and the sound of breaking branches. To try and calm herself, she finally said to the ogre in front of her, "Professor? I was kind of wondering, how come I'm the only student left in class?"

"Hmmm," said the ogre quietly, never breaking his stride. "I'm sure you're aware, Ms. Thistlewhite, that three of your classmates deemed this study to be too difficult and dropped out of the program."

"Yes, Sir," she said quietly. "But the other three, you asked them not to come back." She continued up the path, the sounds of the growling dragon getting louder.

"And?" Slackjaw asked.

"And they were...well, you know...they were so much..."

"Bigger than you," the ogre said, finishing her thought.

"Yeah," Eliza said sadly.

Slackjaw stopped, and once again bent over. "That is true, little Eliza. The others were much bigger than you...physically. But I have a secret to tell you. It's not the size of the dragon in the fight," he winked at her, "it's the size of the fight in the dragon!"

3

hineas Spadeweilder, Phiny to his friends, was small, even by gnomish standards. What was not small, however, was his spirit. Like all gnomes he was born into a family of gardeners. The Spadeweilders were rutabaga gnomes, and none could dig rutabagas quite like young Phiny. He could fill bushel baskets faster than they could be carried away and plant new rows of vegetables quicker than any of the more experienced gnomes. But still, he had bigger hopes and dreams.

He dreamed of being a Crystal Keeper. Magical crystals, harvested from the Forever Cave once a year, were what kept the world of Eden Glen alive and well. No creatures in the Glen were more revered than the Crystal Keeper trolls. The only ones who actually knew where the Forever Cave was located, Keepers were responsible for retrieving the crystals, ensuring their safety for the entire year, and making sure that they were properly rationed out during that time.

Phiny felt that his studies were going well, but he was still very nervous about his oral exam with Professor Cobbletop. Cobbletop the Troll was supervisor for all Crystal Keepers.

Professor Cobbletop, tall and thin even for a troll, looked through the spectacles sitting on the end of his long thin bluish nose. "Mr. Spadeweilder," he began in a surprisingly high and whiny voice, will you please explain to me the significance of the crystals in Eden Glen."

"Of course, Professor," Phiny answered. "Without the crystals, nothing here is the same anymore."

"Specifically?" Cobbletop asked.

"All sources of magic come from the crystals. Our safety. Our languages. Our..." Phiny shrugged his shoulders and looked down at his hands folded in his lap, "...everything."

"I see." Cobbletop leaned back in his chair, stroking his long chin with equally long fingers. "Can you elaborate on that, Mr. Spadeweilder?"

"Well," Phiny said. "We can't talk with each other without the crystals. They make it possible." He sat back, avoiding his Professor's gaze, staring at his own curly-toed shoes.

Professor Cobbletop reached into the pocket of his purple waistcoat, took out a gold pocket watch and consulted it, considered the time, and returned it to his pocket. He smoothed back his thinning white hair, leaned closer to his student, his arms resting on his own knees, and addressed the young gnome. "Phineas, your answers may be correct, but the lack of depth and detail in your answers can be a problem. *Whys and hows* can be just as important as the *yesses and nos*".

He leaned back in his chair again,

stretched his long legs, and tented his fingers in front of him. "Now, Phineas, what say we try some of those answers again."

Phiny let out a deep breath and thought about the answers that he had given. He considered the words that his professor had spoken. He leaned forward, his small hands resting on his brown pant-covered knees. Looking so tiny in the normal sized chair, he tried his answers again.

"Years and years ago, almost before time began, after being chased from the outside world, magical creatures from the whole world were inexplicably drawn to Eden Glen. Everyone was able to live together peacefully, but there was no real friendship or cooperation because no one spoke a common language. All creatures kept to others of their own kind. It was a beautiful, but far from warm, place."

Phiny looked on the wall behind Professor Cobbletop. On it hung a mural depicting the coming together of the many residents of Eden Glen and, for perhaps the first time, he appreciated what the picture was truly saying. Phiny didn't notice the smile beginning to cross the Professor's thin lips, and he continued on, lost in his own story.

"But then one day, the day that humans call the first day of autumn, something amazing happened. Two trolls hunting in the area that we have come to call Mount Autumn, came across a cave that had never been there before. Everyone knows that trolls are the most accomplished of all mountain dwellers, so when they said that the cave had not been there in the past, they were believed. But it was what they uncovered in the cave that was the most astonishing."

Professor Cobbletop looked at his student's face truly enjoying the sense of wonder that crossed it. Quietly in what was really a loud whisper, not wanting to destroy the moment, he asked Phiny, "And what was in the cave?"

"Crystals," he answered. Studying the mural even harder, Phiny realized that while the Forever Cave was the focus of the picture, it was surrounded by many of the early inhabitants of Eden Glen. He noticed that none of the creatures were mingling together.

"Where were the crystals?" Cobbletop prodded.

"Everywhere," Phiny answered. "They were everywhere. No matter where you looked inside the cave, there were crystals. The trolls filled their pockets and brought them to the oldest and wisest troll to seek her council. She wanted to see the cave, but when they returned the next day it had vanished. Not knowing what else to do, the troll elder Glindella sought out the elders of the other groups hoping one of them might understand the meaning. This was the first meeting of what we now call the Council of Elders."

"Yes, yes," uttered Professor Cobbletop. "And then?"

"No one knew what to do with the crystals. It was then that Queen IBeris Candytuft, Queen of the Fairies, held them in her hands and yelled out with frustration, *I wish that we could all just understand each other!*" Phiny sat in the chair clutching his hands in front of him, acting out the scene and not even realizing it. He began to tremble and then threw his hands into the air.

"Suddenly one of the crystals began to shake, flew out of the Queen's hands into the air, and exploded, lighting up the night sky. Sparkling powder settled on everyone and everything. But it was when Corguard the Ogre grumbled the words, *What in the mountain Kings name was that?'* that everything changed. The other elders stared at him in disbelief because they had understood every word he said. When they expressed their surprise they were even more shocked to find that they all understood each other. Queen Candytuft had accidentally cast the spell that we still cast once a year that allows us all to speak to each other in our own languages. It was the real beginning of Eden Glen as a community, not just a place to live."

"Excellent," Cobbletop said, "and after that?"

"Glindella used a second crystal," Phiny said, "to wish a dome of protection around our Valley. Her protection spell is also cast every year, and that is why Eden Glen can only be found by someone who has been here already. The crystals make everything in our world possible."

As he completed his story, Phiny realized that he had been staring at the mural. He understood for the first time the sadness that existed in the early days of the Glen. When he looked at Professor Cobbletop, he was surprised to see a grin had spread across the troll's long thin face.

"Phineas," Professor Cobbletop said while leaning forward in his chair, "you're very smart. That story you just told me proves that. But being a Crystal Keeper is about more than intelligence. It is about the details. Details..., and restraint."

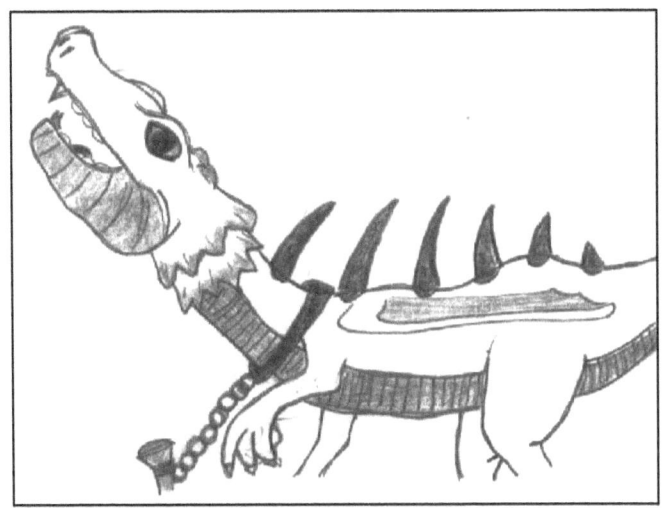

4

liza and Slackjaw entered a clearing in the forest. A high pitched whine filled the air coupled with undertones from the growls of a young dragon. There in the middle of the clearing, being kept in place by a thick chain staked to the ground by a huge spike of oak, was a red juvenile dragon. While certainly not happy, it did not appear to be, at least to Eliza's eyes, in any danger.

"Don't worry, Ms. Thistlewhite," said Slackjaw reading the concern on his student's face. "He's perfectly fine. I only grabbed him this morning. In fact, I even gave him a nice meal. We certainly don't want him to be too hungry for this exercise." The great ogre chuckled deeply, seemingly putting the young dragon at ease.

Eliza knew that it was only a joke, but was still apprehensive at the idea of becoming a midmorning snack for the dragon. Nearly eight feet long from nose to tail, and weighing close to two hundred pounds, she knew that he was small for a dragon. In fact, she could see that he still had most of his milk teeth. He had probably just finished being weaned from his mother, but still, compared to Eliza's mere five inches in height, the dragon was enormous.

"All right, Ms. Thistlewhite," said the ogre, "what can you tell me about our young friend here?"

Eliza looked carefully at the dragon. She fluttered her wings to get closer, and managed not to flinch too badly when it lunged to the end of its chain, trying to get to her. "Hmmm," said the fairy, carefully taking in as many details as she could. "Well, it's a

Bearded Red Spineback Dragon. With only three adult teeth, and none of those being front fangs, I would place his age at less than two years. No damage or wear evident on any of his claws, so I guess he's only been out of the nest for about two weeks."

"Impressive," said Slackjaw. "Anything else?"

"Yes," answered Eliza with an uneasy smile. "Despite what you said, he still looks pretty hungry to me."

Slackjaw laughed out loud. It was a great deep booming sound that echoed through the woods. "Very good, Eliza. It's important to have a positive spirit when dealing with a dragon, even a young one. Now come over here," he said while gesturing where he wanted her to stand, "and see how it's done."

Eliza fluttered to the side of the clearing, trying to get the best possible view of what her professor was about to do. He stepped in front of the dragon and grabbed the heavy chain around its neck. He pulled the dragon's head in front of his own, and fixed his stare into its yellow eyes. The beast immediately fell silent, dropping his head and allowing Slackjaw to begin petting him. The ogre rubbed the nubs that would eventually grow

into the dragon's horns, and muttered soothing words in his deep gravelly voice.

He released the dragon and turned to his student. "All right, Eliza, now it's your turn. Come on over here and give it a try. Remember," he said, patting her shoulder with just his little finger, "your presence and your size are two completely different things." He leaned down, and in his quietest voice, trying to instill confidence in his student, said, "And try to stay calm."

Eliza came forward, taking deep breaths trying to slow down her racing heart. She blotted her suddenly sweating palms on her pants, and willed herself to stop shaking. She fixed her gaze upon the young dragon, and told herself not to blink.

"Any time you're ready, Eliza," said Slackjaw.

Eliza allowed her wings to carry her closer to the beast. He raised his head and looked back into her eyes. He breathed out heavily, causing her hair to flutter. Eliza knew that his breath smelled like brimstone. Some day when he was older, the dragon would be able to breathe fire, but right now he was still too young for that. He cocked his head at Eliza, but she never let her gaze waver. He leaned forward and sniffed Eliza, but she remained strong and never flinched, even when he snaked out his tongue, and pulled her into his mouth!

5

estraint, Professor?" Phiny asked.

"Of course, Mr. Spadeweilder. Why, restraint may be the most important part of a Crystal Keeper's job."

"I'm not sure I know what you mean, Professor," said Phiny.

Professor Cobbletop closed the book in front of them and leaned back in his chair. He removed his spectacles, quickly wiped them with a red handkerchief that he returned to his pants pocket, and then tucked them into a small pocket of his waistcoat. "Let me tell you a little story, Phineas. One you very likely won't find in your textbooks. Those two trolls that found what we now call the Forever Cave may not have been the smartest trolls that ever lived, but they were persistent. Despite all evidence that the cave had disappeared, they continued to go looking for it every night. Finally, one unbelievable night, the cave was there once again."

Phiny shifted in his chair, concentrating on the old troll's story.

"This time," Cobbletop continued, "afraid that it would once again disappear, they took as much as they could possibly carry. When they returned home with their spoils, they showed a younger sister what they had found. Fortunately," Cobbletop chuckled lightly, "she was considerably smarter than her brothers, and much better with numbers."

"You see, she was the one that used her charts and calendars to determine that the cave had appeared on the same night as it had appeared the previous year. She was the one who suggested that it would once again appear the following year, on the very same day. When that day came the three siblings all traveled up the mountain together, but when they got to the cave, it was nearly empty."

Phiny was confused. All of the legends he had read told only of a never ending supply of crystals. "Empty, Sir?"

"Let me ask you a question, Mr. Spadeweilder," Cobbletop said while leaning forward. "When your family, or any gnome family for that matter, harvests the garden, do you remove all of the plants and vegetables?"

"No, Professor, of course not," Phiny answered. "You have to allow some of the vegetables and flowers to go to seed, otherwise there won't be anything to plant the following season." The troll, a light smile playing at the corner of his lips, continued to stare at the young gnome. Suddenly Phiny understood the point that Professor Cobbletop was trying to make. "They took so many crystals there wasn't enough left to generate new ones for the following year. You should only take what you need!"

"Exactly," said the troll, the smile widening on his face. He was very happy to see that his student was finally beginning to understand the finer points of being a Keeper. "There were almost no crystals to retrieve, and the brothers had not been careful about their supply from the previous year."

"They were gone, Sir?" Phiny asked.

"That's right, Phineas," Cobbletop said with a sigh. "The brothers so enjoyed the feeling of importance by giving out crystals, and they were so sure that they had a never ending supply available to them and them alone, they had no crystals left from the previous year. And I have to tell you, Phineas, it caused great problems here in the Glen."

"What kind of problems, Professor?"

Professor Cobbletop leaned forward placing, his elbows on his knees. "I'm sure that you can guess some of the problems, Phineas. After all, you just told me what the crystals allowed life in the Glen to be like. It's fairly simple to imagine what would happen if all of a sudden those crystals were no longer available for use."

Phiny shook his head. It was easy to imagine, and it made him sad to think about it.

"The first of the enchantments to expire

was the one that allowed open communication between everyone. Fortunately," said Cobbletop, "the Council kept the calm. The elders of each group were able to remind everyone that not long before they weren't able to communicate either, and that they would be fine. They called on the younger sister to appear in front of them and she explained, as best she could, what she thought would happen the following year. With her charts and gestures, she explained her idea that the cave would appear on a certain day the following year. She also suggested that if she was told the expected crystal needs of everyone in the Glen for the following year, she could retrieve only what was needed."

"They agreed?" Phiny asked.

"Indeed they did," replied Cobbletop. "As I said, the younger sister was very smart. Unfortunately it would still be nearly a year's time before the cave appeared again. The second enchantment to expire was Glindella's protection spell. The Glen became vulnerable to outsiders, and the Sisters of Darkness were able to enter."

Phiny looked up at his Professor with sad eyes. "The Lacewing family."

"Yes, Phineas, the Lacewings. Had those trolls been more considerate when raiding the Forever Cave, there would have been enough crystals to allow Eden Glen to remain safe. And the Lacewing family would not have been subjected to the curse upon them, but unfortunately that's not how it happened."

"That's amazing," said Phiny. "But how do you know any of this, Sir? I've never come across this story in any of the text or history books that I've read."

Professor Cobbletop leaned toward Phiny conspiratorially. "I'm going to let you in on a little secret, my boy. Those long ago trolls were family of mine. A grandfather, an uncle, and an aunt, all with so many greats attached to them that even I can't count. Those uncles may have stumbled upon the cave haphazardly, but it was my long, long ago Aunt, she that understood restraint and self-control, that became the very first Crystal Keeper."

"Now, Phineas," said Professor Cobbletop, gathering his papers and books. "I believe that it is about lunch time. Why don't you run along? I'm sure that your friends will already be waiting for you."

6

The dragon leapt into the sky, flapping its mighty, leathery wings, spiraling upwards as it fled the clearing. Slackjaw stood off to the side watching it sail away, not saying a word. He quickly and quietly packed the chain in his bag and pried the piece of oak from the ground. The last thing he wanted was for an innocent animal to hurt itself, or become entrapped in his teaching materials.

He slung his pack over his shoulder and quickly surveyed the clearing to make sure that he wasn't forgetting anything. He stepped onto the path in the direction of the school, and slowly trudged through the woods. He walked along silently, never looking back. After five minutes of traveling through the woods he said, "You know, today's exercise wasn't nearly the disaster that you believe it to be."

Eliza, fluttering behind the ogre, dragon saliva still dripping from her body, wasn't sure that she agreed. "I'm sorry I don't feel quite as good about today's lesson as you do, Professor. If you hadn't moved so quickly, I'd be deep in that animal's stomach right now." Eliza continued on, head down, not looking forward. Feeling ashamed, she quietly said, "Maybe I'm not as cut out for this as I thought." She was so upset by her failure with the dragon she did not realize that her professor had stopped on the path in front of her.

Still looking down, she flew right into his belly. She looked up at his face, as he looked down at her. She realized from this angle just how huge and imposing Slackjaw the Ogre really was.

"Eliza," he began, bending down to his student's level. "I understand that you are upset, but you are casting too negative a net over your experience. True, the events that happened were not what we had hoped for, but still, they taught us very much."

Eliza was starting to feel very bad. She was already embarrassed about having to be saved from the dragon by her professor, and now his amusement about it was making her angry. "I suppose," she snapped, "we learned that dragons find me very tasty."

Eliza pouted, crossing her arms, and stomping her foot in the empty air, but that only made Slackjaw laugh harder. "I suppose we did. Next time I should salt and pepper you!" The ogre's laughed deepened, and got even louder, but he put out his hand so his student could alight.

"No, Eliza," he said when he finished laughing. "What we learned is that even when in a dragon's mouth, you were not scared. Why, when I forced that dragon to spit you out, you didn't flee screaming into the woods like anyone else would have. No, not you, Eliza Thistlewhite. You glared at that animal with anger, not fear. And that, my most diminutive student, is the real reason that you are the only one left in this class."

He flipped his wrist, returning Eliza to the

power of her own wings. He straightened up, joined his hands behind his back once again, and continued up the path towards the school. "Now let's get on back," he said over his shoulder. "It's near lunch time, and I'm as hungry as a dragon!"

7

loysius the troll sat on one of the
many rocks in the EGSDK courtyard.
They were arranged in small circles
like benches and tables, and he began to
unpack his lunch on one of them. Most
people would not appreciate a troll's lunch,
but Aloysius' friends never seemed to mind.
When he first began at the Eden Glen School
for Different Knowledge, he never thought
that it was possible for a troll to have friends
that were not trolls, but he was proved very
wrong. After years of eating meals alone, or

only with family members for company, he now loved and looked forward to lunch breaks with his closest, truest friends. That they were all so different is what made them all so very much the same.

Aloysius, just like the other members of his family, had grown up as a bridge troll. His brothers rushed to their calling and had gained reputations as being the best bridge building trolls there were. In fact, *Gort&Shnaud Bridges* was such a successful endeavor, they were booked on jobs for months at a time. Aloysius however, did not enjoy the bridge builder's life. What he enjoyed was sewing and creating with material. He did not build with his brothers; he did, however, design and sew his brothers' work uniforms, and the uniforms for all of their crew.

It was during his second year at the school that a loud, rather annoying little fairy flitted into the sewing room and began pestering him about some very un-fairy like clothing. He made one outfit for her, thinking that now she would leave him alone, but it didn't quite work that way. The next day when he ventured outside to eat his lunch alone as he had planned, he heard his name being yelled from across the courtyard.

"Al. Al! Over here!" It was, to his surprise, the fairy wearing the clothing that he had made, and she was calling him by name with a smile. She flew over to him and grabbed him by his arm. She pulled and tugged as hard as she could, and while there is no way that a fairy, no matter how strong, could pull a troll, he found her persistence intriguing, and went with her.

"C'mon Al," she said, "you have to meet everyone, and they have to meet you. Hey everyone," she said as she dragged him into a circle of assorted creatures. "This is the guy that made my new clothes." That was the first day that Aloysius ever ate lunch with friends, not alone or with family, and it was the last day that he ever wanted to eat alone again.

He began to unwrap a sliced toadstool on mung bean sprout bread sandwich, with dried kale leaves as a side dish, when he noticed a small green bullfrog hopping towards him. The frog hopped onto a rock next to him and blinked its great black eyes at him twice. Aloysius pulled off a small piece of the sprout bread and tossed it toward the frog, which opened its mouth and shot out an improbably long tongue, catching the morsel of food, and

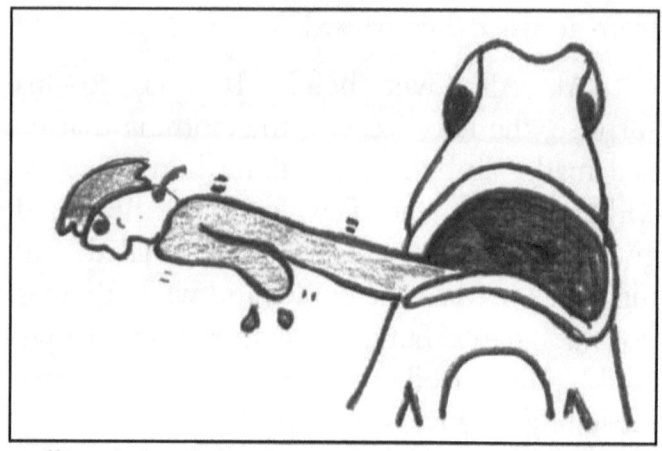

pulling it back into its mouth.

"Thanks, Al," said the frog thankfully when it finished swallowing.

"Never a problem, Miss Penelope," Aloysius said politely. "Did you forget your lunch again?"

"No," Penelope sighed. "It got wet crossing the stream this morning. Things were so much simpler last year when I was a chameleon. I just scampered along the branch line over the stream. I just can't seem to get used to being a frog." Penelope exhaled with frustration, but gladly accepted another piece of sprout bread from Aloysius.

"I wouldn't worry if I were you, Miss Penelope," Aloysius said with a smile. "You always seem to handle these new challenges with vigor. I have no doubt that you will make your time as a frog memorable." He leaned over with a handful of cookies, placing them on the stone in front of her. "Here you are," he said. "It's my mother's own recipe. Water lily macaroons, and they are magnificent."

"Thanks, Al," Penelope said. "You're a pretty great friend."

Penelope Lacewing had a less than easy life. In the early days of Eden Glen, during the time when Glindella's protection spell had expired, the Sisters of Darkness were able to enter the enchanted valley, and wreak havoc. Eventually they were driven from the Glen, and the dome of protection was restored, but not before a wicked enchantment was placed upon the Lacewing family. Now, when any member of the Lacewing family celebrated a birthday, they woke up not as the fairy that they were meant to be, but as a different reptile or amphibian. Having just celebrated her birthday, Penelope had only been living as a frog for two weeks.

"Hey, Big Al," said Phiny as he approached the circle, carrying an oversized lunch pail. "Hey, Hop-a-long!"

"Is that supposed to be funny, Shorty?" Penelope answered.

"Aww, come on, Penny," said Phiny. "Don't be upset."

"It seems, Phineas," said Aloysius, "that Miss Penelope finds herself without lunch today. We all know that no one prepares like a gardening gnome, so I am sure that you must have a little bit extra in that lunch pail of yours."

"Of course I do," he said while searching through his lunch pail. "I'm pretty sure I saw some boysenberry biscuits in here, and I probably have some extra potato thins as well." He stood up with small bags in each hand. "Would you like some?"

"Thanks, Phiny. I appreciate it."

"Not a problem, Pens. Hey," he said looking up from his sandwich, "has anyone seen Eliza? I'm dying to find out how her first lesson with a real dragon went." He began eating his lunch unaware that Eliza had walked up behind him. Phiny sniffed the air and asked, "Hey, does anyone else smell brimstone?"

"Good afternoon, Eliza," said Aloysius as he cleared a spot for Eliza to sit down. "How did you fare in this morning's class?"

"Seriously, guys," asked Phiny, "do you smell brimstone?"

Eliza gave Phiny a sideways stare and then turned back to Aloysius. "I've certainly had better classes. I'm starting to think that I made a mistake studying dragons. I'm just not sure that I'm up to it."

"Come on," said Phiny angrily. "Someone has to smell that!"

"IT'S ME!" Eliza yelled while stamping her tiny fairy feet. "I smell like brimstone! I smell like brimstone because that is what dragon's spit smells like. And I smell like dragon's spit because... THE STUPID DRAGON ATE ME!"

"I knew I smelled brimstone," muttered Phiny as he turned back to his lunch.

Eliza's shoulders slumped and tears began to roll from the corners of her eyes. With a big sniff and a sigh, she lifted her chin. "I just have to try harder. I'm the only one left in that class, and I will not quit!"

"Good for you, Eliza," Aloysius said clapping his hands. "Anything I can do to help, I'll be glad to do. Oh, by the way, Phineas, mum asked me to thank you for that bushel basket of rutabagas you sent over. There is no better dessert than my mum's creamy rutabaga pie."

"Not a problem, Al," replied Phiny, as he popped a couple of potato thins into his mouth. "My parents were thrilled that your brothers were able to fix that bridge in our back field. It was making dad crazy not being able to get across the stream and tend the back garden. Now that dad can get to the beets on the other side, he's going to drop a bucket over at your house. But don't tell your mom, he wants it to be a surprise."

"Excellent," said Aloysius as he handed water lily macaroons to all of his friends. "I hope I'm home when he comes by. I'd love to measure him. I have an idea for a new style of pants especially for gardening gnomes. They'll have extra pockets, padding sewn into the knees for getting down in the dirt, and extra loops around the waist to hang tools from. I'd like to make a pair for him to try."

"Cool! I'm sure he'd like that," Phiny said, taking a bite from the cookie. It was a bit more bitter than he would have liked, but he didn't want to offend his friend so he slipped the rest into his mouth.

"So, Phiny," said Penelope, "did your big oral exam go better than Eliza's morning?"

"I'm not so sure." Phiny turned towards Penelope, and gave her the last of his rose petal jelly on crackers. "I'll admit it didn't start very well, but I think it got better. Then something really weird happened. Professor Cobbletop started talking to me. Not a lecture like usual, but talking to me, like a friend. He even told me a story about the very first Harvest Day that I had never heard before." Phiny shrugged his shoulders. "It was strange."

"Did he eat you?" Eliza asked, her mouth

half full of a sandwich she didn't particularly want.

"No."

"Then your day went better than mine," she said, the beginnings of a smile pulling at the corners of her mouth.

Her smile disappeared quickly however when a blue bird with a piece of paper in its beak flew down to the center of the group. It dropped the paper in Phineas' lap before flying away. He read the note and looked at Eliza with worried eyes. "It's from Dean Shodbottom. He wants to see the two of us in his office. Right now!"

8

liza and Phineas stood in front of the main school building, staring up at the improbable tower that stretched high above the ground. It did not stand straight up and down like most towers, but leaned to the left and then back to the right, defying gravity and all logic. At the top of the tower they could see a curl of white smoke rising from the chimney. There was a fire burning in Dean Shodbottom's office, which would make it feel even warmer than it already was.

"Any idea what we did wrong, Eliza?" Phiny asked.

"I don't know what you did," said Eliza. "But I'm sure that the Dean heard about how badly I screwed up this morning. I've wasted almost two years of Professor Slackjaw's time. He's going to throw me out of school for sure."

"No way," said Phiny. "If anything he's going to toss me out. My big exam and all I did was give one word answers. Did I tell you that Professor Cobbletop even had to stop the exam to tell me how bad my answers were?" Phineas shook his head sadly. "I think he was disappointed in me, and he's the head Crystal Keeper for all of Eden Glen. I'm done."

The two began the long climb up the twisting, winding staircase. Both tried to comfort the other, presenting logical reasons why the other would be safe.

"Come on, Phiny. You know more about the Forever Cave, crystals, and how to harvest them than anyone I've ever met." Eliza tried to boost her friend's spirits. "You even know more than the books that I tried to read. You'll be just fine."

"Maybe, Eliza," said Phiny, "but you're a superstar around here. You're a fairy that takes on dragons. Even Slackjaw is a little afraid of you, and he's not afraid of anything."

"Phiny," Eliza said, "he had to reach into a baby, not an adult mind you, a baby dragon's mouth just so he could pull me out." Eliza shook her head as the two friends continued to climb the stairs. "He's not scared of me, he's annoyed by me." Eliza sighed as they reached Dean Shodbottom's door. "I guess bunnies aren't that bad. I just thought that I was destined for so much more."

"You are, El. I may not know much else, but I know you're heading for greatness," Phiny said, patting his friends shoulder. "And when you get there, I'm going to be right at your side."

Phineas reached up to knock on the heavy oak door, but before he could swing his hand a voice called out from inside.

"The door is open, kids," said the voice. "Come on in."

Phineas pushed against the heavy wood,

and it swung open easily on the well-oiled hinges. Eliza and Phineas, already nervous about the meeting, immediately felt the heat of the fire on their faces. The walls in Dean Shodbottom's office were covered on three sides with floor to ceiling bookcases. Tomes and textbooks on any conceivable subject were there. Considering the average gnome's minuscule height, sliding ladders mounted on brass rails adorned the bookcases. Phiny and Eliza wondered if he even knew what the books on the top shelf were, or if he ever climbed the ladders to read them.

The fourth wall, behind the Dean's desk, held a doorway leading to a small balcony. It was rumored that the view from the Dean's balcony was the most amazing view in all of Eden Glen. Even the Council of Elders room in the top of the Meeting Tree could not compete with the view that Dean Shodbottom had. The rest of the wall was covered in oil paintings of various size, shape, and age.

Some paintings held images of great figures in the Glen's history. Some showed important and historic moments that helped make Eden Glen the amazing place it was. And some showed figures that were not

famous, but for reasons known to the Dean, and maybe only the Dean, were very important to him. In the center of the wall however, right at the perfect eye level for a gnome, was something that was not a painting at all.

In a simple wooden frame, mounted under glass, was a single sheet of paper. Strange curled writing ran across it (you or I would certainly recognize it as English). Eliza couldn't understand the writing, but knew that the Dean had brought it back from the human world, as a souvenir.

Neither Eliza nor Phineas could see the Dean. They were both too short to see over the great cherry desk at which he sat. They could only see the top of his pointy red hat shaking ever so slightly while he wrote with a great plumed pen. Never looking at his two students, he tipped the feather toward three tall chairs arranged in front of his desk. "Have a seat, kids. I'll be with you two in just a minute."

Phineas and Eliza sat in two of the chairs. Curious about the third, they remained silent. The scratching of the Dean's pen on his paper was making the two nervous students even more anxious. Dean Shodbottom finally finished his writing, replaced his pen in its holder, and sealed the letter with a generous dollop of wax. He finally turned his attention to Eliza and Phiny.

"All right then, the reason I called for you was..."

"We're so sorry, Dean Shodbottom!" Eliza blurted out almost immediately.

"We'll try even harder!" Phiny yelled. "Please don't kick us out."

The Dean sat staring at his two students with complete surprise. He looked from Eliza's face to Phiny's, and then back again. He thought he saw tears starting in both of their eyes, and had to fight with himself to keep from chuckling. "I'm not sure what brought that on, but I want to assure both of you that I have no intention of asking you to leave. What could possibly make you think that I would?"

Eliza wasn't sure what to say. She didn't want to lie to the Dean of the school, but she also didn't want to tell him about her morning's events if he did not already know. "You haven't spoken to Professor Slackjaw, Sir?"

"Well of course I have, Ms. Thistlewhite. Speaking with our institutions' teachers about our students is a very important part of being the Dean." The Dean hopped down off his chair and walked around to the front of the massive desk. He hoped being on the same level as his two students would help them feel more at ease. He grabbed a small chair and sat down with them, leaving one chair empty.

"In fact, when I first accepted the position of Dean here at our fine institution, I decided to experience some of our classes. I thought it would help me better understand the challenges that some of the students faced." The Dean leaned over closer to Eliza. "I remember the day Slackjaw took me into the woods to face my first dragon. When it roared, I jumped out of my curly shoes and almost wet my pants." Both Phiny and Eliza laughed when he said that, and the Dean winked at them with a smile. "I dare say you handled yourself much better today than I did."

"And as for you Mr. Spadeweilder," he said turning his attention to Phiny. "I've been led to believe that you better understand crystal history, Keeping philosophy, and crystal location than any student that Professor Cobbletop has ever had. I dare say you two are the prize students of your teachers." Dean Shodbottom leaned back in his chair and gently stroked his white beard. "It's too bad you two don't believe in yourselves nearly as much as your professors and I do."

Eliza and Phineas looked at each other, then back at the Dean. Both turned a slight shade of red, embarrassment from their outbursts. "We're sorry, Sir," said Eliza. "We just thought that we were finished here at the school."

"If I can ask, Sir," asked Phiny, "why did you want to see us?"

"Oh yes," said the Dean, clapping his hands together with a laugh. "You two got me so distracted, I'd completely forgotten. I have a special project that will be perfect for you and your friends."

Eliza immediately brightened up. She saw a chance to redeem herself, and was very eager to please. "You've got the right group for the job, Sir." She jumped from the chair and started making her way toward the door. "We won't let you down."

"Uh, Eliza," the Dean said.

Eliza stopped before walking out the door, and turned around, a flush of embarrassment on her cheeks again. "I forgot to find out what the project was, didn't I?"

"Yes, you did," said Dean Shodbottom with a smile. "But I love your spirit, Ms. Thistlewhite." The Dean nodded toward the still empty chair and said, "I'll tell you what the project is as soon as our last guest arrives."

The three of them sat chatting about nothing special. They discussed their studies, friends, and life at the school in general. Suddenly there was a knock on the heavy door, and Dean Shodbottom said, "I believe that's the young lady we've been waiting for. Come in," he called.

When the door opened, a young blond elf

walked through the door. Dressed in a purple jacket with an oversized leather book bag over her shoulder, she cautiously entered the office. A set of eyeglasses sat unevenly on her upturned nose, the temples tucked behind her pointy ears. Dean Shodbottom hopped down from his seat and greeted her at the door.

"Welcome, welcome," he said taking her hand. "You didn't have any trouble finding the office did you? No? Wonderful." The Dean led the young elf to her chair and began the introductions. "Eliza Thistlewhite, Phineas Spadeweilder," he said gesturing to the two students sitting in the chairs, "I would like to introduce you to Jocelyn Bartleby. Ms. Bartleby has just joined our school, and her area of study is why I wanted her to work with your group. Her knowledge should prove invaluable in your assignment."

"Pleased to meet you Jocelyn," said Eliza, reaching out to shake her hand. "It should be fun working together. You'll like our friends too, but I'm not sure what it is we'll be doing together. We haven't been told yet."

"What is your course of study, Jocelyn?" Phiny asked.

"It's nice to meet both of you," she said with a smile, "but please, my mother and my grandmother are the only ones who call me Jocelyn. All my friends just call me Beanpot." She dug into her bag and pulled out a sketch book full of her original drawings. "I'm sure you know that we elves are famous for our work with legendary beings. I've actually chosen to follow this course of study as well, and I can't really learn anymore at home. That's why I'm here."

"That's why indeed," said Dean Shodbottom. "Ms. Bartleby's father is one of my oldest and most revered friends. He has sent young Jocelyn to us with a problem to address, as well as to try and further her education. Let's all have a seat, and we can discuss the problem, and how we can begin to resolve it."

9

veryone," began Eliza as they returned
to the courtyard, "I'd like you all to
meet Beanpot Bartleby. Beanpot, this
is everyone." Eliza introduced Aloysius and
Penelope to Beanpot, and then huddled them
all together.

"You guys won't believe this," said Eliza.
"The Dean has given the five of us a special

assignment. I'll let Beanpot tell you all about it. It's really a little more of her specialty."

"Thanks, Eliza," said Beanpot. She began to unpack her drawings and other notes. "Okay, there are a lot of creatures and beings that most people believe to be imaginary."

"You mean like abominable snowmen?" Penelope asked.

"Actually," replied Beanpot, "they're not abominable at all. They are interesting and quite friendly when you get to know them."

"Seriously?" Penelope said with surprise.

"Yes," Beanpot answered. "We elves have spent our lives studying and helping to protect creatures that most think are just legends. The reason my father sent me here was to help recruit Dean Shodbottom to help us with a very serious issue. There's a problem with the last unicorn."

"Unicorns are real?" Aloysius asked.

"They are," said Beanpot. "Unicorns are given life by the belief in magic by human children. For reasons none of us can quite figure out, human children just don't believe in magic anymore. And now the last unicorn is in trouble."

"What's wrong with it, Beanpot?" Penelope asked.

Beanpot sighed and found a scroll with the drawing of a young unicorn from her bag. "As you can see here," she said pointing to the drawing, "when a unicorn is healthy, its horn is a sparkling rainbow of color. It shines like the Sun and inspires belief in magic." The group studied the drawing while Beanpot continued. "The last time we saw the last unicorn, its horn had turned gray, and it did not look healthy. That was almost two months ago."

There was a tear in Beanpot's eye. "We

have no idea where it is, or how to help it. If it dies before a new unicorn is born, they will stop existing. Forever."

"What do you need us to do?" Eliza asked.

"To be honest, I'm not really sure," said Beanpot. "All I know is that we need to find it. Let's all head home, and maybe I'll come up with something by tomorrow."

10

Unfortunately, none of them had any great ideas. They continued to look in the forest near their homes, and of course they talked to all of their relatives. They spoke with everyone who lived along the forest's edge, but sadly they were no closer to finding the sick unicorn. Despite their searching, their studies continued, and they were all doing well.

Aloysius had given Phineas' father his

64

new pants, and he loved them. In fact, he loved them so much, half of the gardening gnomes in Eden Glen had ordered a pair. Aloysius' Tailoring Professor had given him an "A" based solely on the positive reviews of the gnome community.

Penelope had enrolled in the Legendary Beings program with Beanpot, and was doing quite well. When Beanpot found out that Penelope was a member of the famous Lacewing family, she insisted that Penelope join her class.

Eliza had two more classes with a live dragon, and while she wasn't eaten either time, she still hadn't managed to control one. And Phineas continued his one-on-one studies with Professor Cobbletop. He was learning more about Crystal Keeping than anyone, other than a troll, had ever known.

Phineas and Professor Cobbletop stood behind the school facing the small pond which students studying the care of water birds used for their training area. Professor Cobbletop inhaled deeply, relaxing his body in the warm sunshine and spoke to Phineas in a calm voice. "Mr. Spadeweilder, tell me when we harvest the crystals."

"Of course, Professor," answered Phiny

as he turned his face towards the sun. "The cave only appears on the day that humans call the Autumnal Equinox. The day that summer turns into autumn in the human world."

"That is correct, Mr. Spadeweilder." Professor Cobbletop turned towards Phiny, raising his hands toward the horizon. "Now, Phineas, what can you tell me about the seasons here in Eden Glen?"

"Well," Phiny thought for a minute. "The seasons don't come one after the other like they do in the human world. In the outside summer follows spring, autumn follows summer, and so on. But here in Eden Glen the seasons exist next to each other, all occurring at the same time, just in different areas." Phiny raised his arms and spun around slowly. "The school is here in Summer Meadows." He pointed to the left into the distance and said, "That is Mount Autumn, and the trees are always in various shades of reds, yellows, and oranges. Way off in front of us," he said as he moved his hand, "is the Winter Cliffs. It's always frozen over and snow covered. But I have to say, my family took a quick vacation there last year, and the sledding was a lot of fun."

Professor Cobbletop nodded and smiled. "And finally?" he asked.

"Finally, off to the right is Spring Fields," Phiny said. "Spring flowers are always in bloom, and it is a favorite place for fairy families to live. My family lives here in Summer Meadows, just like most gnome families." Phiny smiled proudly to his Professor. "The best vegetables always grow here in Summer Meadows."

"Very good, Phineas," said the professor, patting his student on the back. "Now, there's something I want you to be thinking about. I want you to consider the unique calendar we live by here in Eden Glen. The harvest time is almost upon us, and in the outside world autumn will arrive in just one days' time."

Professor Cobbletop and Phiny began gathering their papers and books. The class had come to an end for the day, and the professor had a meeting that he needed to get to. As he started to walk away he called over his shoulder, "I will tell you this though, Phineas. I am planning on doing something I've never done before."

"What's that, Professor?" Phiny asked, trying to catch up.

The tall troll looked down at Phiny and smiled. "Well, I was thinking about inviting my best student to join me for the harvest."

"Wha... Wha... What?" Phiny couldn't believe his ears. He was sure that he had misheard his professor.

Professor Cobbletop laughed out loud, heartily. "That's right, my boy. I'd like you to join the other Crystal Keeper and I. I feel very confident in your progress, and I think this will be a great opportunity for you to further your knowledge about crystals."

***

Phiny saw Eliza coming out of the woods, trailing behind Slackjaw, and ran excitedly toward her shouting, "Eliza! Eliza!" When he got closer to her, he stopped short, realizing that the giant ogre was looking down at him. He immediately looked down at his feet, afraid to meet Slackjaw's iron gaze. "I'm sorry, Professor. I didn't mean to interrupt your lesson."

Slackjaw smiled down at him and said, "That's all right, young man. As a teacher here at the school, it's hard to be upset at enthusiasm." Turning to Eliza he said, "You're excused, Ms. Thistlewhite. I hope you kids have a nice day." Slackjaw laced his hands behind his back and walked away. It was hard to believe of such an imposing and scary figure, but he began to whistle a happy song.

"Is he...," Phiny asked, pointing after the ogre.

"Yes, he is," said Eliza. "Quite often, actually."

"But he's...,"

"I know," Eliza sighed, "a big scary ogre. But he's a big scary ogre that likes to whistle. Now, would you mind telling me what's so important that you're interrupting the end of my class?"

"I'm so sorry, El," Phiny apologized. "It's just that I'm so excited. Professor Cobbletop actually asked me to join him on Harvest Day! Can you believe it?"

Eliza threw her arm around Phiny's neck and squealed in his ear as she hugged him tight. "Oh Phiny, I'm so happy for you! Can you believe that just a few months ago, you and I both thought we were getting thrown out?

"I know, I know," said Phiny. "It seems so silly now. No student has ever...actually, no one, has ever been invited on a crystal harvest. If this goes well, I'm almost guaranteed a job in the Keeper's Office when we graduate."

"I am so proud of you, Phineas Spadeweilder," said Eliza very formally while holding him at arm's length. "You really are making your dreams come true."

"Awww, knock it off, El," he said, twisting out of her arms with a smile. "You sound like my mom when you do that. But thanks." He looked at his friend and saw that her eyes were not entirely happy. He put his hand on Eliza's shoulder, and with concern asked, "How did your lesson with the dragon go this morning?"

"Not as great as yours, I'm afraid," Eliza said sniffing back a tear. "I thought I had him for a moment. I stared into his eyes and he was nice and calm, and then I must've done something wrong. All of a sudden he reared up and tossed me at the end of the tether."

"Are you okay?"

"Physically? Yeah." Eliza shrugged her shoulders and sat down. "Maybe I really should quit, I just keep screwing up. Maybe everyone was right. I'm just too small to control a dragon."

Phiny put his arm around Eliza's shoulder, as the two of them walked back to the school. "No way. Not possible. You'll get it, I'm positive. If I know anything, it's that you are going to be the best dragon fairy ever."

Eliza couldn't help but laugh. "Phiny, I would be the only dragon fairy ever."

He leaned back, a huge grin spreading across his face. "See what I mean? The best! And I will have been there from the very beginning."

"Thanks, Phiny," Eliza said hugging him. "I really needed that."

Suddenly they heard their names being called from across the courtyard. "Eliza! Phiny! There you are, I've been looking everywhere for you!" Beanpot was running across the grass towards them. She was waving frantically and pointing at the tower at the top of the school. "We have to get to the

Dean's office right now."

"What happened?" Eliza asked, jumping forward.

"I just saw a falcon fly into the Dean's office window," said Beanpot. "My father always uses falcons to send messages. That's how he sent word to the Dean about the unicorn problem in the first place." She grabbed Eliza and Phiny's arms, and began to drag them toward the main school building. "It's a message from father, I'm sure of it. Let's go."

As the three of them started off quickly towards the Dean's office, Aloysius came rushing out of the textile building. "Thank goodness I found you three. I've been looking everywhere."

"We're off to the Dean's office, Al," Eliza said. "Can this wait?"

"No, it can't," Aloysius said. "I think I know where the unicorn is!"

11

"You what?" Beanpot asked, sure that she had misheard him.

Aloysius was very excited and was speaking very fast. Eliza had to grab his hand, tell him to take a deep breath, and to speak more slowly. "My father," Aloysius said, still out of breath, "has been off in the Winter Cliffs helping my brothers build a new bridge over Iceflow River. He returned early this morning and I overheard him telling my mother about a strange horse he saw. He told her he thought it was injured because he believed it had a grey branch stuck in its head. He said he tried to help it but couldn't get close enough before it ran into the woods."

"Do you think that could have been the unicorn?" Phiny asked.

"I'm sure it was," said Beanpot worriedly. "The reason Aloysius' father didn't recognize it as a unicorn was because he doesn't believe that they're real."

"So we're headed to the Winter Cliffs?" Phiny asked.

"Not necessarily, Phineas," answered Aloysius. "Dad said that he saw it while he was traveling home. He said the 'horse' was heading in the direction of Mount Autumn."

"Hmmm," said Phiny.

"What are you thinking, Phiny?" Eliza asked.

"I'm not sure, El. It's not really anything, just sort of an itch on my brain," said Phiny. "It might not be anything, but let me think about it a bit. When it makes sense to me, I'll let you know. I promise."

"Fair enough," said Eliza.

Beanpot reached her hand up as a blue bird swooped down toward the group. It dropped a piece of paper into her hand, and soared back into the sky. She unfolded the note and quickly read. "Just as I thought, guys, the Dean wants to see us. Now."

***

The four of them stood in the Dean's office. Aloysius had just told him about his father's return this morning, and Dean Shodbottom was pacing the room, wringing his hands. "Oh dear, oh dear," he said with concern. "This isn't good at all."

"Excuse me Dean," said Eliza quickly. "Isn't this good news? We know the area that the unicorn is in. We can leave in the morning."

"Eliza," said the Dean. "You don't understand all of the facts. Ms. Bartleby's father has sent me a very urgent message. That is what I actually wished to discuss with you children."

"What did my father say, Sir?" Beanpot asked.

Dean Shodbottom turned to Beanpot, and sat wearily in his chair. "My dear, your father and his people have done some

figuring. According to them, the unicorn has less than two days to live."

The group of students gasped in horror.

"And that may not be the worst of it," added the Dean. "They also believe that the unicorn's magic level has dropped so low, it's now in danger of being eaten by a dragon." The Dean jumped off his chair and headed to the door. "No, no. You kids are done with the unicorn now. I have to think of your safety." He pulled the heavy wooden door open, and as he stepped into the hall said, "I'm sorry, I need to call Slackjaw. He may be the only one that can help us now."

***

They walked down the stairs from the Dean's office sadly. Beanpot finally broke the silence. "I guess we just go home and wait.

It's too bad, really. It was fun when we were doing something that felt important."

"Don't worry, Beanpot," said Eliza. "I'm not done with anything. You guys get home and pack some travel bags, then meet me at the stables."

Beanpot, Aloysius, and Phineas all froze on the stairs, watching Eliza continue down. Suddenly she spun around, a hard determined look in her eyes. "Let's go!" As she continued down the stairs, she said, "I'm not letting that unicorn die!"

12

A loysius arrived at the stables to find that Eliza, Beanpot, and Penelope had already arrived. "So, Miss Penelope," he said while fastening his bag to the horse's saddle, "will you be joining us on our fool's journey?"

"Not tonight, Al," Penelope replied. "I'm not sure how helpful I'd be to you guys in this condition anyway. Besides, someone has to stay here that knows what's going on. I'm going to keep doing as much research as I can, and if I learn anything, and I mean anything that I think will be helpful, Beanpot's leaving me her father's falcon. I'll get a message to you guys as quick as I can."

"Thanks, Pens," said Eliza while hugging her friend. "I don't know what we'd do without you."

"Hey, what's with the hugs?" Phiny asked as he entered the stables. "You guys are all acting like we aren't coming back from this little adventure, but my mom is making maple coated Brussels sprouts for dinner tomorrow night. No way that I'm missing that." He went over to Eliza, and put his hand out to her. "Here you go, El, it was the only piece of crystal that I could come up with."

"Thanks, Phiny," Eliza said as she took the piece of crystal, and handed it to Penny "That should be perfect."

"Well, don't get too excited," he said clipping his bag to the horse's saddle. "When Professor Cobbletop finds out that I stole it from his office, plus I don't show up for the Harvest trip tomorrow, I'm probably getting tossed out of school for real this time."

"Phiny…," said Eliza, feeling guilty about asking him for the favor.

"It's okay El," Phiny said, shrugging his

shoulders. "Does your dad need a bunny apprentice?"

Beanpot leaned forward and kissed Phiny on the cheek. "I'll never forget what all of you are doing to help me. Ever."

Phiny blushed and looked down at his shoes. "Geez, can we please get going before I change my mind?"

"Okay, hero," Eliza said with a smile, "let's get going. Okay, Penny," she said leaning off the horse and looking down. "Do you really think this will work?"

"Of course it will work, Eliza," said Penelope.

She took the crystal and rubbed it slowly on the hooves of the two horses. The horses stood still, but began to breathe heavily and swing their tails. "I may look like a bullfrog, guys, but I'm still a horse fairy at heart. You four better mount up quick, the horses are starting to feel the magic."

Phiny, Eliza, and Beanpot sat on one horse, while Aloysius sat on the second. No sooner had they sat in the saddle and grabbed the reins, they felt the horses beginning to tremble. When they looked down to make sure that Penelope hopped clear, they noticed

that the horses' hooves were sparkling.

"Hold on tight, you guys," yelled Penelope as they galloped out of the barn. "They'll run twice as fast with that speed enchantment." She hopped to the stable door and as the horses thundered across the field into the distance, she yelled, "Good luck!"

Penelope began to head back to the school and her research when Professor Cobbletop and his associate entered the stables. "Why, Ms. Lacewing," the Professor said, "what a surprise it is to see you here this evening." He looked around for a moment and then said, "Uh, where are our horses?"

13

The four friends and their magically enhanced horses sped through the night beneath a clear and starry sky. The moon was just past its full phase, and it cast an eerie ghostlike glow over the land. Despite the bright light however, it was still difficult to see the uneven ground. Fortunately, Penelope's enchantment made the horses as sure footed on the uneven terrain as a dancer on stage.

"So which direction do we head in?" Aloysius yelled.

"Winter Cliffs," answered Eliza.

"Where it leads to Mount Autumn," said Beanpot.

"Actually," said Phiny, "I've been thinking about that. Remember that thought I had earlier? I think it's a real idea now."

"Okay, Phiny," said Eliza, "let's hear it."

"I'll tell you," said Phiny with a smile. "But don't be too upset with me if it sounds a little bit like a history lesson. I've been thinking about this ever since that talk I had with Professor Cobbletop about the beginnings of life here in Eden Glen. Everyone was drawn here, but no one knows why. I mean, think about it. The troll families didn't call the fairy families and say, "hey let's go here." Yet, they all showed up here anyway."

"All right," said Eliza. "That's a good point."

"Then the troll brothers found the Forever Cave," said Phiny. "It was the end of the growing season. They shouldn't have been anywhere near the cave, but they were."

"Another good point," said Beanpot, "but what does it all mean?"

"Well," said Phiny, "what if they were drawn to the cave? You know, the magic called to them?"

"Is that even possible?" Aloysius asked.

"I don't really know," answered Phiny. "It's just an idea I have. But what I'm really thinking is that we should be heading towards the Summer Meadows side of Mount Autumn. I'm willing to bet that the unicorn is being drawn to the cave and the crystals."

"That makes sense actually," said Beanpot. "Al's dad did say that he saw it heading in that direction. But if that's what's happening, how do we find the unicorn, or the cave?"

Phiny's smile grew a little wider. "I've been thinking about that, too. When the Professor asked me to think about the human calendar and the Glen's geography, he told me to think about the two of them together. I began to realize that Eden Glen is laid out like a giant calendar."

"What?" the three friends asked all at the same time.

"Really," said Phiny. "Think about the calendar that they use in the human world. If you imagined the dividing line between Winter Cliffs and Spring Fields being the equivalent of what humans call the Vernal Equinox, then the border between Summer

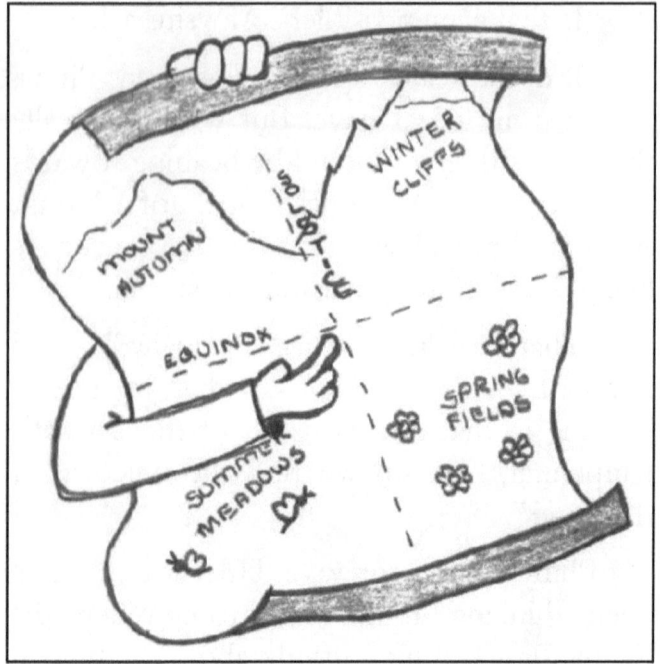

Meadows and Mount Autumn would be the Autumnal Equinox. That's the day on a human calendar that the cave appears here in Eden Glen. That means that's where the cave is, somewhere near the border!"

The friends all looked at each other, and finally Eliza asked "Everyone agreed?" They all nodded their heads. "Good. We'll follow your plan, Phiny. Your idea is the best I've heard so far, and let's be honest, you're the expert on the subject."

They pulled slightly on the reins and veered the hard charging horses toward the border of summer and autumn. They continued on in silence for a short while when Eliza quietly said to Phiny, "You know it's a very, very long border. How do you expect to find the cave?"

"El," Phiny said, "when we get close enough, I think the cave will find us."

***

As they rode Phiny finally said, "Beanpot, I've really been dying to ask you a question."

"Okay," she said, "ask away."

"Why Beanpot?" Phiny asked.

"Wow," Beanpot said as she began to giggle. "That's a kind of long story."

"Well," replied Phiny, "it's a kind of long ride."

"When I was a baby," Beanpot said, "my family traveled. I mean they traveled a lot. We were always moving from one place to another. My mother told me that one day I was crying but she couldn't hold me and hold the reins of the horses pulling the wagon at the same time, so she put me in the family's old bean pot on the seat next to her. I guess I fell asleep, and when my dad who was driving the other wagon saw me, he thought it was very funny." She shrugged her shoulders, "I've been Beanpot ever since."

Hours into their journey, as the sun began to rise over Summer Meadows, the four friends finally entered the foot Hills to Mount Autumn. They slowed the horses to a trot, and scanned the horizon for anything that would help them. There was no sign of the unicorn, and according to Phineas' figuring, it was still an hour before the cave would become visible. They continued their trek toward the border following Phiny's directions.

"I think we need to head a short way up the mountain," Phiny said. "Not very far up, but the cave will be somewhere inside the tree line. That would help keep it hidden."

They were making their way up the beginnings of the incline when Phiny climbed down from the saddle of the horse. He took a deep breath and tried to clear his thoughts. He stretched out his arms, turned his face slightly, and began to slowly turn in place.

"Phiny?" Eliza asked.

"Shhh!" Phiny said impatiently. "I'm trying to feel the crystal's pull, just like the unicorn is."

He continued to spin very slowly, finally stopping while facing to the right of the horses, and those seated upon them. "I think it's in that direction. I don't know why, but it feels like the right way to go." He reached into his pocket and removed a gold pocket watch, a gift from his grandfather the day he enrolled at the EGSDK. "Just forty minutes to go, come on."

"Hey, Beanpot?" Phiny asked as they began making their way through the bushes and trees.

"Yes, Phiny?"

"There's something else I've been wondering," said the young gnome. "Why isn't your father out here hunting for this unicorn instead of us?"

"He's not here, Phiny," she answered.

"You mean he's not here on Mount Autumn?" Phiny asked.

"No, Phiny," she said quietly. "He's not here in Eden Glen."

"He doesn't live in the Glen?" Eliza asked.

"No." Beanpot suddenly looked very sad. "My family lives in the outside world, that's why he sent me here. My parents are members of the group that are still fighting dark magic in the world. After we save the unicorn, they're expecting me to rejoin them."

They all considered that they were going to lose a friend when their adventure was over, and that Beanpot would lose all of her friends when she left. They did not have a chance to think about it for long though, as the air was torn by the fierce roar of an adult dragon.

14

Looking up, they were just able to make out the shadow of an enormous dragon soaring over their heads. While they watched it head to the left of them, they heard the screech of the Bartleby family falcon. It swooped low enough to drop a rolled up piece of paper in Beanpot's lap. She opened it and read quickly to herself.

"It's from Penny," Beanpot said. "She said she found some old writings in gnomish that refer to curing a sick unicorn. The story told of a blackened horn being brightened with a stone of great particularity. She doesn't think that just any crystal will work. She says we have to find a specific crystal, but that should make the unicorn better."

"Sounds simple enough," said Phiny. "Anything else we should know?"

"Um…let me see," Beanpot said as she read over the note again. "She doesn't say what the special crystal is, I guess that's going to be your job, Phiny. But she did say that whoever saves the unicorn receives…, Let me see what she wrote. Ah, here it is…, 'A magic that if in light, shall be more powerful than if in dark.' I'm not quite sure what that means, but it won't matter if we don't find the unicorn."

Phineas checked his watch again. "Only ten minutes to go, and I'm sure we're going in the right direction."

They heard the dragon roar in the distance again, and felt chills run up their spines. They moved forward, then Phiny told them to stop.

"What's wrong?" Aloysius asked.

"We're here," answered Phiny.

"How can you be so sure?" Eliza asked.

Phiny pointed towards the edge of the clearing. "Look," he said. There, laying on the edge of the clearing was a now mostly grey unicorn.

They all ran to its side as Phiny asked, "Are we too late?"

"No," said Beanpot. "She's still breathing, but barely." Beanpot glanced over her shoulder, and suddenly opened her eyes wide. "Phiny! Look!"

While they were all huddled around the unicorn, the Forever Cave had appeared in the clearing. Aloysius turned to his friends and said, "There's not much time. Phineas, you and Eliza get in that cave and figure out which crystal we need, Jocelyn and I shall attend to our ill friend here. Please hurry."

***

Phiny and Eliza entered the Forever Cave wide-eyed and in amazement. Crystals of every size and color sparkled around them. Every direction they turned in, they were awed by the beauty of the cave. Phiny studied all of the crystals, searching for the one that he wanted, while Eliza just stared.

"Phiny," she said, "we could just..."

"NO!" Phiny said firmly. "We can't Eliza. The cave will know." Remembering what his Professor had taught him, he said, "Restraint is important in these situations. We take only that which we need, and I think I see it right over there."

Phiny walked across the cave floor, Eliza following behind him. "Hey, El," he said, "remember the drawing that Beanpot's father sent? The healthy unicorn's horn is all rainbow sparkles." He bent over, and using his pocket knife, carefully removed a crystal from the wall. Eliza looked at the crystal in Phiny's hand, and it shone brightly, every shade of the rainbow twinkling within it. He handed it to Eliza and said, "Go. That poor unicorn needs you to save her."

"But, what about you?" Eliza asked.

"I think I'm just going to look around in here for a moment," Phiny said sadly. "I've waited nearly a lifetime to see this place, and I have a feeling I'm not getting invited back again."

***

Eliza emerged from the cave and ran directly towards Beanpot, Aloysius, and the unicorn. She fell to her knees at the animal's head and held the rainbow crystal in her hands. "What do I do, Beanpot?" Eliza asked.

"I'm not really sure, Eliza," she answered. "I've only read about these kind of things, I've never actually done it."

"I may be wrong," said Aloysius, "but it seems to me that the most logical thing to do would be to apply the rainbow crystal to the horn that should be rainbow colored."

"Sounds good to me" said Beanpot.

"Give it a try."

Eliza carefully touched the crystal to the unicorn's horn. Almost immediately the crystal began to sparkle and tingle in Eliza's hands. As the friends watched, the colors began to seep into the unicorn's horn. Her grey ashy color began to lighten, and with her head on the animal's chest, Beanpot could hear her heartbeat strengthen. As Eliza continued to hold the magic crystal to her horn, the unicorn lifted her head and they were able to see, for the first time, her deep blue eyes. As the unicorn began to stand, Eliza fluttered her wings, never allowing the crystal to break contact with her horn.

After a few moments the crystal, though still glowing, held no color at all. The unicorn, however, was beautiful. Her horn shone with the colors of the rainbow, and her mane flowed freely over a brilliant white body. She leaned down and nuzzled her nose against Beanpot's cheek. She lifted her head and did the same thing to Aloysius. When she raised her head to Eliza, who was still fluttering her wings in the air, the unicorn used her nose to push the crystal in Eliza's hands closer to her tiny body. Eliza stared into the unicorn's blue eyes, and as a tear came into her own eyes, she

said, "You're welcome."

The unicorn turned away from the friends and plunged into the bushes, bounding away. Eliza wiped the tears from her eyes as she fluttered down to settle next to her friends.

"I do believe, Miss Jocelyn," said Aloysius, "that your father will be rather pleased with your next report."

They all began to laugh. The incredible tension that they had been under while searching for the unicorn had washed away now that it was healthy, and they just laughed.

"Did I miss something?" Phiny asked as he walked out of the cave.

"You sure did, Phiny," said Eliza between

breaths. "Al made a joke."

Suddenly Beanpot stopped laughing, her face quickly turning very serious. "Eliza! I get it."

"You get what?" Eliza asked. "You mean Al's joke?"

"No, not that," said Beanpot. "What Penelope wrote to us about. It's the crystal!"

"What are you talking about Beanpot?" Phiny asked.

"That crystal in her hands," she said pointing at Eliza. "There shouldn't be any magic left in that crystal, but look at it. It's shining brighter than ever."

"You mean…?" Eliza asked.

"Yes!" Beanpot said. "I mean that is the reward. You saved the unicorn, you get the big wish. But," she said as a warning, "it has to be a good wish, not a bad one. 'In light, not dark'."

Phiny jumped up and down excitedly. He reached out and grabbed Eliza by the shoulders. "This is it, El! You can wish yourself into a dragon fairy. It's your dream come true."

Before Eliza could answer her friend, they

heard a rustling and crashing sound coming toward them from the bushes. Suddenly Fognoggin the Troll, Assistant Crystal Keeper to Cobbletop, came storming into the clearing. He looked at the children for only a moment as he ran past, yelling in his high squeaky voice, "Get in the cave! RUN!"

The four friends looked at each other confused. Phiny finally asked, "What just happened?"

Before anyone could offer him an answer, Cobbletop ran into the clearing, stopping in front of them, clearly shocked by their presence. He looked at them and was about to speak when a great roar came from the woods very near to where they were standing. Cobbletop quickly reached out to the students and pushed them towards the mouth of the Forever Cave. He spoke only two words.

"Move! Dragon!"

15

hen they were all safely inside the cave they peered out into the clearing. The huge dragon crashed through the trees and bushes and emerged into the open. It violently thrashed its tail, pounding it to the ground, causing the floor of the cave to tremble under their feet. The dragon swung its huge head, sniffing wildly, trying to locate the prey that it had been chasing. Cobbletop put his hands on his knees and leaned closer to Eliza. "Ms. Thistlewhite," he said, "I must confess, I am at a complete loss as what to do. I have never encountered a dragon in these woods at Harvest time. What can you tell me about it?"

Eliza fluttered a bit closer to the mouth of the cave. Staying close to the rocky entrance, she looked carefully at the huge snorting beast. "Well, it's a Green Crested Finback. Unfortunately, it's one of the most dangerous dragons you can come across. I'd say it's about forty feet in length, nose to tail, and nine feet tall at the shoulders. And if I had to guess, it weighs in at just less than ten thousand pounds."

"None of this," said Cobbletop, "is making me feel any better, Ms. Thistlewhite."

"This won't help then," added Eliza. "See those long tendrils growing from the dragon's chin?"

"Yes," said the troll," I do now."

"The length of those tendrils tells me that we're looking at a full grown dragon, and it has been on the hunt for some time now." Eliza sighed, allowing her wings to let her settle to the ground. "We may have to just stay in here and hope that it gets bored and leaves."

"What?" Phiny yelled. "We can't!"

Cobbletop looked at everyone with a very worried expression. "I think what Phineas is trying to say, is I'm not sure that is going to be an option. As I'm sure Phineas could tell you, and I still can't believe that you kids are here, this cave is only here for a short period of time. If the time comes for this cave to disappear, and we are all still inside…, I have no idea what will happen to us."

"Eliza," Beanpot said stepping forward. "There's only one real option. Use your crystal. If you wish yourself into a Dragon Fairy, then we'll all be saved."

"What crystal?" Cobbletop asked.

"It's a long story, Professor, and don't worry about my wish. I've already made it." Eliza stuffed the crystal into her backpack and slung it over her shoulders. She tightened her hands into fists at her sides and took a deep breath. As she exhaled she allowed her fingers to relax. She turned toward the whole group. "Phiny, I never would've made it this far without you. And Al? Thanks for humoring an annoying little fairy. I love you guys."

She turned towards the opening of the cave, listening to the continued roaring,

crashing, and spitting from the clearing. "Professor," she said to Cobbletop, "our horses are tied to trees not far from here. You five need to finish the harvest. Eden Glen is counting on you. Leave the dragon to me." She turned and fluttered out of the cave.

As Eliza exited the cave, the dragon noticed her. It turned around and rose onto its hind legs menacingly. The others looked on from the entrance to the cave, terrified for her safety. The dragon lunged forward, mouth open, directly at Eliza, but she easily dodged out of the way. It roared in frustration, and blew a fire ball in Eliza's direction. She flapped her wings hard and spiraled away from the flame. The dragon swung its huge head at Eliza, snapping its mighty jaws, trying to bite down on the tiny fairy.

As the dragon tried to snap its teeth shut around Eliza, she fluttered backwards just enough to avoid their closing. She could smell the strong odor of brimstone, and felt the wind caused by its closing mouth so very close to her small hovering body. Eliza did not however take the opportunity to fly away, but instead reached out with both hands and grabbed hold of the long tendrils growing from the dragon's chin. It began to snap it's head, but Eliza pulled tightly, and fixed her hard gaze right into the dragon's yellow eyes. After only a moment, the dragon relaxed and lay down quietly. Eliza released her hold on its tendrils, and patted the beast's snout gently.

Eliza hopped onto the dragon's neck, and turned toward the cave. She saw the amazed expressions on the faces of all those inside. She yelled out to them, "Remember, the Glen needs those crystals. I'll send back some help, but I have something that I need to do right now." She leaned down and ran her hands up and down the dragon's neck. "Okay, girl," she whispered in the animal's ear, "let's go."

Beanpot, Aloysius, and Phiny ran out into

the clearing just in time to see the dragon soaring away with Eliza riding on its back. "Phineas!" Professor Cobbletop called from inside the cave. "You three better get back in here. We don't have much time." The three of them ran back to the cave, each taking a burlap sack from Fognoggin as they ran through the entrance. Cobbletop put his hand on Phiny's shoulder and said, "And you're going to need all of that time to explain to me just how you got here."

***

Eliza looked down breathlessly at Eden Glen. Soaring as high as she was on the dragon's back, she wondered if anyone had ever seen the Glen the way that she was seeing it now. As they flew over the school, the dragon roared, announcing its arrival and she decided that this view was even better than the one from Dean Shodbottom's balcony. Eliza continued farther, finally bringing the dragon down in the center of Spring Fields, in front of the Lacewing home. She jumped down to the ground and patted the dragon's long nose. "All right, girl," she said, "just wait here."

As Eliza approached the front door it flew open, and Penelope hopped out. "Oh Eliza," she said, "you did it. You figured out the clue, didn't you?"

"I sure did, Pens," Eliza said with a big smile.

"And you used your wish to become a Dragon Fairy," Penelope said with a tear in her eye. "I'm so happy for you."

"Actually, Pens, I did use my wish," said Eliza as she took the glowing crystal out of her backpack. She tossed it to Penelope saying, "I just used it on something else."

When the crystal hit Penelope's hands it began to sparkle and tremble. Penelope began to feel strange in her body and looked at Eliza. She yelled, "What's happening to me?"

Penelope's parents, a gecko and a skink, came running out into the front yard. "Penelope!" they both yelled, "What's happening to us? We feel all tingly."

Suddenly the crystal exploded in Penelope's hands and the dust swirled around the Lacewing family. They slowly lifted off the ground in a sparkling cloud of crystal dust. A crowd had gathered in the town square, first drawn to the arrival of the giant dragon, but now unable to take their eyes off the scene in front of the Lacewing's home. As the dust

settled, instead of two lizards and their bullfrog daughter, stood a family of horse fairies. A lifetime long curse had been lifted by the selfless wish of a true friend. A wish that was made not in darkness, but in light.

When the Lacewings looked at each other and realized they stood in their true form, they embraced each other tightly. Applause broke out among the fairy community of Spring Fields, and all rushed forward to share in their friends' joy.

Eliza merely smiled, leaning back against the dragon's snout, watching the excitement unfold. "You know, girl," she said gently rubbing the animal's nose, "I think that was even cooler than I hoped it would be."

16

A great throng of gnomes, fairies, and trolls had gathered at the foot of the meeting tree. The annual address from the Council of Elders, often to discuss the success of Harvest Day, always drew a large crowd. But the unusual events on this year's Harvest Day made the address something that none wished to miss. While many bumped and pushed to get to the front of the crowd, many others tried to get closer to the celebrities of the day.

Some wished to speak with the young fairy that had flown the largest dragon ever seen into the center of town. Others wished to speak with the young gnome that managed to find the one place that generations of creatures had searched for and been unable to find. And some wished to speak with the mysterious elf, new to Eden Glen, who had led the group to find and save the last unicorn.

The large brass bell near the top of the meeting tree rang out signaling the beginning of the address. The crowd quieted and turned their attention to the lowest branch. From a hollow opening in the giant tree, the Council of Elders stepped out onto the low hanging branch which had a large speaking platform built on it. Greycrest the Troll, the most senior member of the Council, stepped forward, raising his hands to the crowd.

"Citizens of Eden Glen," he began in a deep and booming voice. "Thank you for joining us today. I have spoken to Head Crystal Keeper Cobbletop, and he has assured me that the Harvest was a great success." A roar of applause came from the citizens in attendance. Greycrest raised his hands again to quiet the crowd. "And Slackjaw the Ogre has assured me that the dragon has been returned to its natural habitat, and there is no danger at all." Another roar of applause came from the crowd. "In short my friends, life shall continue to be wonderful here in Eden Glen for another year. Thank you all for coming."

As quickly as it had begun, the address was over, but everyone's concerns were eased. People started heading home, or off with friends and things began to return to normal. As Phineas, Eliza, and Beanpot began heading toward the school they noticed Aloysius and Penelope standing off to the side. The friends came together in the center of town square. "Well," Aloysius began, "I must say, it has been quite a couple of days."

The group all began to laugh. "I can't believe it, Al," said Phiny. "All this time I've known you, and now, you get a sense of humor." They continued to laugh, but their laughter stopped when they saw professors Cobbletop and Slackjaw standing together looking at the group. Phiny and Eliza walked over to their teachers.

"I must say, Phineas," began Cobbletop, "you certainly surprised me these last few days. I'm still a little unclear about some of the details of your adventure, but perhaps we can discuss them better tomorrow."

"Tomorrow, Sir?" Phineas asked. "I don't believe we have a class scheduled for tomorrow, Sir."

"No Phineas, not in class," replied Cobbletop with a smile. "At the Crystal Keepers Office. Fognoggin has decided that being chased by a dragon is a good reason to retire, and I now find myself in need of a new assistant."

Phiny stared at him wide-eyed. He couldn't speak, afraid that he was misunderstanding Cobbletop's words. "So…"

"Yes, my boy," said the troll laughing. "The job is yours, if you would like it."

Instead of speaking an answer, Phiny jumped forward, throwing his arms around the much taller troll's legs. "Oh thank you! Thank you! Thank you!"

Cobbletop separated himself from the young gnome, turned and started to walk away. "We have a lot of work to do. See you promptly at eight o'clock…Phiny."

***

"How do you like that?" Eliza asked.

"Seems about right to me," answered Slackjaw.

"So…," said Eliza. "See you tomorrow, Sir?"

"No, Eliza, you won't," answered the ogre. "I have a class in the morning. A new group of students is starting."

"Yeah," said Eliza, trying not to show her disappointment. "I understand." She turned away hoping to keep him from seeing her tears.

"However, Eliza," Slackjaw called to her as she walked away. "I'd love for you to stop by the class sometime next week. It will do the new students well to see that with hard work, what a successful dragon handler they can become." As he turned to walk away, the huge ogre winked and smiled at Eliza.

As their professors walked away, Phiny and Eliza just stared at each other. Suddenly they began jumping up and down and screaming with joy. Aloysius, Beanpot, and Penelope joined them in their celebration "I'm so happy for the two of you," said Beanpot. "I just can't believe that I'll be leaving soon. I'll miss you all so much."

"Actually," said Penelope, "I've been meaning to talk to you about that. Everyone," she said to the group, "I have an announcement to make. I'm leaving Eden Glen."

They were all shocked. "What do you mean you're leaving?" Aloysius asked.

"Dean Shodbottom and I have been talking," answered Penelope. "He helped me contact your father, Beanpot. I really am enjoying the study of legendary beings you introduced me to, and your dad pointed out that I've spent my entire life as a legendary being. He has invited me to work with him in the outside world, and it's an opportunity I don't want to give up."

With tears in her eyes, Eliza hugged her friend. "I will miss you so much, but I'm so proud of you."

"Aw, come on, El," said Penelope. "I'll write all the time, and if I get in any trouble out there, who do you think I'm going to call?"

"Well," said Beanpot, "at least someone is coming home with me."

"Actually," said Penelope. "Your dad thinks that you should stay here a bit longer. Dean Shodbottom's told him about the friends that you made, and he thinks that your education here at the school is a little more important."

Eliza squeezed one of Beanpot's hands,

and Aloysius squeezed the other.

"That sounds just like Uncle Jeremiah," said Beanpot.

"Uncle?" Phiny asked.

"Yes, Uncle," Beanpot said. "My mother's brother. Didn't I ever tell you that my mom is a gnome?"

"Let me get this straight," said Phiny. "You're part gnome?"

"Mm-hmm," said Beanpot with a nod and

a smile.

"And you're staying?" Phiny asked, a silly grin spreading across his face.

"Oh boy," said Eliza, pulling Phiny's hat down over his face. "I think he's in love."

They all laughed, and Phiny blushed a bright red, but when Beanpot reached down to hold his hand, he didn't pull it away.

"Come on everyone," said Aloysius. "Let's head over to my house. Phiny's father dropped the bushel basket of turnips off this week, and you'll love what my mother did with them."

The End....for now...

ABOUT THE AUTHOR

Bruce lives in Peabody, MA with his wife and fellow author Nadine, and their two beautiful children. He is hard at work on his next *Eden Glen Chronicles* adventure, as well as a new and exciting escapade for Katie and Steven Calabash as well as Babru the Pirate.

www.ingramcontent.com/pod-product-compliance
Lightning Source LLC
Chambersburg PA
CBHW030545130626
46552CB00006B/2425